For Harriet ~ M.P.T.

To my mom, my dad, and my brother,
for giving me the best childhood
I could ever have ~ H.G.

tiger tales
5 River Road, Suite 128, Wilton, CT 06897
Published in the United States 2021
Originally published in Great Britain 2021
by Little Tiger Press Ltd.
Text by Maudie Powell-Tuck

ISBN-13: 978-1-68010-264-2 • ISBN-10: 1-68010-264-8
Printed in China • LTP/2800/3727/0521

2 4 6 8 10 9 7 5 3 1

www.tigertalesbooks.com

FSC
www.fsc.org
MIX
Paper from responsible sources
FSC® C017606

The Forest Stewardship Council® (FSC®) is an international, non-governmental organization dedicated to promoting responsible management of the world's forests. FSC operates a system of forest certification and product labeling that allows consumers to identify wood and wood-based products from well-managed forests.

For more information about the FSC, please visit their website at www.fsc.org

THE MAGICAL CHRISTMAS STORE

by Maudie Powell-Tuck   Illustrated by Hoang Giang

tiger tales

Benji's grandma had always said, "Magic happens on Christmas Eve."

This Christmas needed some magic. There wasn't enough money for a tree or even a turkey, and everyone felt a little sad.

Benji passed dazzling stores and excited shoppers. "I wish I could buy my family spectacular presents," he sighed. "That might make them smile again."

But Benji's grandma was right about Christmas Eve, because when he turned to go home . . .

. . . a ginormous polar bear ran right into him.

"I'm sorry!" the polar bear cried. "I'm late for work!"

Benji scrambled to his feet and gasped . . . .

A huge, glamorous store had appeared,
shimmering in the frosty air.
"This way, sir," said penguin doormen, tipping their hats.

Benji blinked
at the sky-high
Christmas tree,
the snow falling
lightly from the
ceiling . . . .

"It's real magic!" he marveled.
And for the first time that Christmas,
Benji felt excited.

TOOT TOOT!

A shiny steam train puffed around the corner.
"Hop on," grinned the polar bear.
"Let's find those presents!"

They raced along a golden track, spiraling higher and higher! Benji's head spun with candy canes, lights, and sparkly ornaments.

All too soon, the train stopped.
"Here we are. The room of
silly sounds," said the polar bear.

BOING! POOOWEEE!
YUMMA YUMMA TING TONG!

Hana would love this! Benji thought.
It was crazy and loud, and it would make her laugh.

Benji blew a funny-looking, twisted trumpet.

"FLIPPERTY FLAARP!"

"Excellent choice, sir!" enthused a flamingo. "Your sister will be thrilled."

"But I can't afford it," said Benji.
"I only have a few dollars."

"Dollars?" trilled the flamingo.
"We don't want your money.
Sing us a song instead.
The sillier, the better."

Benji sang the silliest song he knew and had everyone in stitches.

"Good-bye!" Benji waved. "Thanks for the trumpet!"

"Who's next on your list? Your grandma?" asked the polar bear. "We have to find something VERY special for her. Next stop . . .

. . . the room of imaginary gifts!"

It was pretty empty. "There's nothing here," said Benji.

"Sir has to use his imagination,"
drawled a leopard store assistant.
Benji closed his eyes, imagined hard,
and then opened them again . . . .

The room bulged with extraordinary gifts. Genie lamps, treasure chests, bejeweled suits of armor . . . . But these weren't right for Grandma.

"It has to make her feel wonderful," said Benji.

Then he saw it: a most magnificent imaginary hat. "How much, please?" he asked.

"One exceptional story," said the leopard, packing the hat in a box. So Benji told the finest tale he could imagine and left the leopard purring with contentment.

The final present was for his dad. It had to be just right, Benji explained.

"Sometimes my dad feels sad that he can't buy us very much. So when he opens my present, I want him to feel happy. I want him to feel . . ."

"Loved?" asked the polar bear.

The polar bear took Benji's hand and led him into a room filled with fabulous smells, like cinnamon, chocolate, and crackling fires.

"Try this," said the polar bear, opening a jar labeled "Excitement." Benji sniffed, and

WHOOSH . . .

he was zooming along a roller coaster.

"Let's try another!" he laughed.

One sniff of a jar labeled "Summer Vacation," and he was on a beach, breathing in the salty air!

They smelled jar after jar, all amazing, but none was quite right for his dad — until the last one. It was a small jar labeled "Joy." Benji sniffed . . . .

It smelled like family movie night on the couch, like walks together in the fall, like a hug from the person you love most in the world . . . .

Benji left the store with his bag heavy, his head full of magic.

"Good-bye, good-bye!" waved the polar bear.

Back home, Benji couldn't stop looking at the presents.

"Someone is excited for Christmas," said Grandma at dinner.

Hana and Benji woke up very early the next morning.

"It's Christmas!" Hana yelled.

Grandma made a special breakfast, and then they decorated Dad with garland.

But when it was time to pass out the presents, Benji paused.

He had an empty hat box, a twisted trumpet, and a small jelly jar.

These presents weren't spectacular! They were terrible!

But then Hana laughed as she blew her trumpet, and Grandma pranced around the room in her new hat, trilling, "Darling, I've never felt so wonderful!"

Dad sniffed the jar and beamed. "It's wonderful, Benji!"

Everyone hugged. Benji had given them the best presents money can't buy.

They all felt happy. They all felt loved. And Christmas was magical once again.